Bobby Normal
And
The Fallen

A.S.Chambers

Dedication

A huge thank you to everyone who kindly backed my Kickstarter campaign for this book. Special mentions go to
Stephen Logan,
Charlotte Smith,
Nadine Shinfield,
Charlie,
Debs,
Ron Chick,
Becka Pearce,
Rebecca "Boo" Hardy,
Simon Brindley,
Rebecca Armstrong,
A Holmes,
Rohanna.

Also, special thanks to the members of my Patreon Book Club for their valued support:
Kevin Denwood,
Jacob Matts,
Paul Lewis,
Gemma Innes.

For more details about my Book Club and how you can receive signed copies of my books when they are published, please visit my website:
www.aschambers.co.uk.

Also a huge thank you, once again, to Liam Shaw for his amazing cover art.

Ebook short stories.
High Moon - 2013
Girls Just Wanna Have Fun – 2013
Needs Must - 2019

Novellas.
Songbird – 2019
Bobby Normal and The Eternal Talisman - 2021
Bobby Normal and the Virtuous Man - 2021
Bobby Normal and the Children of Cain - 2022
Bobby Normal and the Black Dragon - Due 2024
Child of Light - Due 2023
Child of Fire - Due 2025

Omnibuses.
Children of Cain - 2019
Macabre Collection: Volume One - 2022
Macabre Collection: Volume Two - 2023
Sam Spallucci Omnibus: Volume One - 2022

CONTENTS

Previously...

Bobby, a teenage boy from Irlingbury, and Katy, his fiery eight-year-old sister were entrusted to deliver the Eternal Talisman to a man called Jason, who was believed by his followers to be the Virtuous Man, the individual who could bring about the fall of Kanor and save humanity from the perils of the Divergent Lands.

With the help of a curious old man called Cutter, the two orphans did as they were asked. However, a plan that Jason had concocted to destroy a troop of constructs, the mindless clay golems of Kanor, failed disastrously and he blamed the children, ordering them to be burned at the stake as traitors.

Just in the nick of time, Bobby and Katy

were snatched from their awful fate by Claw, Tigress and Scorpion, three vampires known as the Children of Cain. On returning to Irlingbury, the orphans discovered that their home village had been destroyed and its inhabitants slaughtered. They decided to travel with their new friends. As they did so, Claw told them how he was searching for the true Virtuous Man; someone he believed to be his old friend from before the Divergence, a person named Sam Spallucci. Tragically, during a battle with the fallen angel Asmodeus and a cohort of his constructs, Tigress and Scorpion were killed and Claw was badly wounded. As the children waited for the vampire to recover, the old man Cutter appeared and revealed that he was, in fact, the Shadow Wraith that had murdered the orphans' father.

Chapter One

Fire was a peculiar thing, Bobby thought to himself as the object of his musings spat and crackled in front of him. On one hand, it was a force of devastation, reducing buildings and their occupants to pitiful ash in just hours. He and his sister Katy, who sat aggressively poking this particular blaze with a long stick, had borne witness to this fact just three days ago when they had returned home to Irlingbury and found it burned to the ground, all human life eradicated. However, it could also be a source of safety, burning bright to keep any manner of fierce predators at bay, and a source of comfort, a reminder of the hearth at home for someone journeying through the barren wilds of the Divergent Lands.

The teenage boy stared across the burning wood at the creature that sat opposite. There was no way that it needed protection from hungry beasts and it certainly would not have any warm, fuzzy recollections of a home, a family. The creature that pretended to warm its hands by the campfire had no heartbeat, had no pulse; it did not require the heat from the flames. It certainly had nowhere to call home, having been fashioned from the very clay within the ground itself for one purpose alone: to kill without remorse all those who stood against Kanor, the Black Dragon, the devastator of humanity.

Just as it had Bobby's and Katy's father.

The youth swallowed and tossed a stray piece of wood onto the fire. He cast his eyes up towards the waning crescent of the moon above and blinked back salty tears.

When the Shadow Wraith that they knew as Cutter had arrived, pandemonium had briefly erupted. Claw transformed into a blur as he streaked across the small clearing only to come to a sickening halt with his neck in the firm grip of the construct. Katy screamed at the monster to let their new friend go as the vampire, still weak from its battle with Asmodeus, batted feebly at the creature's arm. Bobby saw red. He snatched up the Child of Cain's silver-tipped whip and the long weapon cracked out across the night air as it flicked around the construct's outstretched arm. The Shadow Wraith turned to the boy, a look of sadness on its face, and immediately transformed back into its old man form.

"Bobby," it said, "we need to talk." Then, gently, it lowered Claw to the floor and released its grip.

That had been a while ago now. Unable to muster up any kind words, Bobby had turned his mind to practicalities and had built the campfire around which all four parties were now seated. He lowered his eyes from the watchful moon and glared at the old man. "You wanted to talk, so talk."

The Shadow Wraith that looked like an elderly man tamped down a wad of smoking mixture into the bowl of his old pipe and ignited it with the end of a glowing stick that he took from the fire. "I'm guessing… that you know who I am," he said between puffs.

"You killed our father. In front of me."

The construct nodded. "That I did, and that action has haunted me ever since."

A sharp tutting noise came from Claw's lips. "A construct that feels remorse? You'll forgive me if I'm sceptical."

"There are more foolish things in which to put one's faith."

"Such as?"

The construct turned its head towards the vampire. "The belief that Sam Spallucci is your *Man of Virtue*." Bobby could not fail to recognise the disdain in the creature's words. "Spallucci is long dead and there is no virtue in this land."

"On the former, I beg to differ; on the second… Well, we have your kind to thank for that, don't we?"

Bobby frowned. "Claw's right. I've never met a construct that feels guilt. Why should you be any different?"

The monster in the form of an old man shrugged. "In short, I don't know. I have spent the last five hundred or so years doing what has been expected of me with no hesitation, no remorse. All of that came to a crashing halt when I killed your father. It was as if the hand of some unseen force had been thrust into my chest and had squeezed a beat out of my still, clay heart. My mind was transported back to my moment of creation. I was standing in All Saints looking upon Kanor and all I felt was revulsion and loathing, at both my creator and my centuries of actions."

Claw frowned. "You say that Kanor fashioned you?"

Cutter nodded.

"But the Shadow Wraiths are Asmodeus' *toys*."

"I was the very first. The Fallen may lay claim to our invention, but we, and the method of our creation, were gifts to him from the Black Dragon." He gave a darkly amused chuckle. "You really think that self-important narcissist would spend time studying how to improve the deadliest weapon on the face of the planet? Let's face it, he didn't even create the original model in the first place."

"You're talking about Asherah," Claw mused. "Back in Ancient Egypt."

Cutter gave another small laugh. "Indeed it was." He raised a questioning eyebrow. "Have you met the female Fallen?"

"Once, in passing. It was a very long time ago. *Eventful* would be the best description of how things turned out." The two long-lived beings sat silent for a while with their memories. Eventually, Claw asked, "So why are you here?"

The old man turned to the two children that he had made into orphans. "Bobby, Katy, you must not follow Claw on his quest for the Virtuous Man. It is folly."

"Why should we believe you?"

Three sets of eyes, one human, one vampire, one construct, turned toward the eight-year-old girl. It was the first time that she had spoken since Bobby had made the campfire and her small voice cut across the still night air. Bobby reached out and lay his hand on top of hers.

"I have committed possibly the worst crime to a child that a being can. I robbed you of your parent, causing you to have to fend for yourselves in this cruel world. Eventually, I found the courage required to try and atone for that sin and I followed you when you set out on your quest with the Eternal Talisman. I decided there and then that I must not let any more harm come to you. This is why I cannot hold my peace right here, right now. I say again that the man that he," Cutter pointed to the vampire with the mouthpiece of his pipe, "is looking for does not exist. Spallucci is dead. There is no Man of Virtue." He held up a gnarled hand as Claw opened his mouth to protest. "Your father was a good man. Not only that, he was influential. He was part of a growing movement that was rising up against Kanor. Removing him from the equation was supposed to squash that rebellion flat before it gathered momentum. However, your involvement with the disastrous shenanigans of Jason and your encounter with Asmodeus yesterday will ensure one thing and one thing alone, you will have been noticed.

"Kanor's forces will come for you."

"I will protect them," Claw protested.

Cutter drew deep on his pipe and blew

out a long stream of smoke. Once again, he pointed the long implement at the vampire, swaying the mouthpiece from side to side: "And how did your last encounter with a Fallen work out for you? No, these children should come with me. I can protect them better than you." His voice softened. "It is the least that I can do."

"Katy," said Bobby, "what do you think?"

The light of the fire danced in the young girl's eyes. "I'm tired," she replied. "I want to go to sleep." And, with that, she curled up in front of the campfire, pulled a blanket over herself and closed her eyes.

Bobby ran his fingers through his sister's hair. "We need to think about this. Let us sleep on it. We'll decide in the morning."

Cutter nodded.

"In the meantime," the boy continued, "I think it would be best if you left us for now. I think I speak for both of us that we find your presence somewhat unsettling."

For a moment, Bobby thought that the Shadow Wraith would protest, but instead, it rose to its feet, nodded and walked away from the clearing, leaving the tired children alone with their vampiric companion.

Bobby's sleep was far from restful. Sharp flashes of fleeting images caused him to toss and turn on the hard-packed ground.

To begin with, the dreams were warm and comforting. Images of his father drifted before his eyes: the kind man fashioning a leg for a chair, his strong hands gliding a plane along the smooth wooden surface; his father sat resting in his armchair, gazing into the crackling hearth; his father cradling an infant Katy in his arms and running his callused fingers through Bobby's unruly mop of hair.

But they soon took on a darker, more disturbing feel. The screams of his mother dying in childbirth; his father being led away by Teller's father; his father dying at the end of Cutter's arm.

As his father died in front of him, Bobby screamed out and all the onlookers of the barbaric execution turned to face him expectantly. They stood and stared at him as if waiting for him to act, looks of puzzlement on their faces.

All except one.

An old woman pushed her way through the crowd, leaning heavily on a stout, weathered walking stick, the hue of which was not too dissimilar to her old, wrinkled face, tanned by many years' labour under a harsh sun. As the rest of the crowd stood agape, motionless, she paused in front of Bobby, leaned on her stick and peered at him. As she did, Bobby could not help but gasp. Her eyes were unlike any that he had ever seen before. They contained no irises or pupils but were a mass of swirling water, small flashes of fire cascading within their azure depths. As he peered into those depths, he felt as if he were drowning and all around him the waters were singing in a three-fold melody. His head swam as he was lifted beyond the skies, far beyond the stars to which humanity had longed to travel so many centuries ago. He was carried up on the lilting tune that mingled with his blood, pumped his heart at such a rate that he thought the organ would explode, before being settled back down in a wide green field where a solitary oak tree stood sentinel. The old woman stood before him, but she was not alone. On her left stood a woman the age his mother had been when she had died; on her right a girl not much older than himself. Both of them looked at the confused boy with the same swirling watery eyes as the old crone.

As three, they nodded in agreement.

"This one," the old woman smiled, "will do."

Bobby awoke with a start, his hands flailing around his blanket, reassuring himself that none of what he had witnessed had been real. He was still in the small clearing. Claw was seemingly asleep on the other side of the fire, enveloped in his voluminous cloak which would protect him from the rays of the sun that were creeping over the horizon. Katy was...

Gone!

Bobby snatched back his sister's blanket and saw just flattened grass. He pressed his hand to the ground. It was still warm; she could not be far. The boy momentarily glanced over to the sleeping vampire but decided that his fiery sister had probably gone off in a huff. As such, she would need a gentler, more knowing hand to rein her back in. He rose to his feet and saw that she was not out in the open marshland where they had battled the constructs, so set off following the path in the other direction.

Chapter Two

Bobby found that it wasn't exactly hard to follow the route that his sister had taken. It appeared that the irate eight-year-old had spent as much time hitting out at random bushes and patches of weeds as she had stormed off on her own to goodness knew where. Bobby couldn't help but smile as he saw first one plant thwacked in half, then another. He imagined Katy chuntering to herself as she whipped a make-believe wooden sword first one way then the next, striking down imaginary opponents that dared to get in her way.

There, was an annoying older brother: thwack!

There, was a mysterious vampire: chop!

There, was a deadly construct: hack!

Here, was a circle of adults who kept telling her she was *too young*: crunch!

As a result, it wasn't very long before he caught up with her.

The affronted sibling was stomping back down the route along which they had travelled to reach the Rishton wetlands. The current focus of her ire was a small sapling that definitely looked like it was now no longer going to grow into any form of a majestic tree.

The image of the large, elderly oak from his dream flashed into Bobby's mind and he shoved it away. He had more important things to deal with now rather than bizarre trees and surreal, watery-eyed women.

"Katy!" the teenager called out as he ran towards her. "Wait for me!"

The small girl stopped beating seven bells out of the offensive foliage and resumed her strident march away from the campsite. "Go away!" she called out without even looking back. "Leave me alone!"

Bobby paused briefly to roll his eyes

then resumed his running. He quickly caught up with the irate girl. "Where are you going?"

"Home."

Bobby sighed. "Katy, it doesn't exist anymore."

"Then I'll start again."

"What with?"

"I'll improvise."

"They burned everything. It's just ash and cinders."

"I'll find a way."

Bobby changed tack. "Why didn't you wake me?"

Katy ignored the question and carried on stomping down the beaten-up road.

"Katy, I asked…"

"I heard you."

"Well?"

The small girl abruptly drew to a halt and Bobby had to prevent himself from colliding with her back. "Because you'd have stopped me."

"And why would that be a bad thing?"

Katy momentarily glanced back the way that she had come. When she turned to face Bobby, he saw that her eyes were wet. "I… I liked Cutter," she stammered, fighting back the tears.

"So did I."

"He killed Dad."

Bobby nodded.

"We trusted him. How can we trust *any-one*?"

Bobby sighed and knelt down on one knee, bringing himself to his sister's eye level. He reached up and thumbed a tear away from her cheek. "I don't know," he admitted. "Everything seems so… so… complicated." His final word was expelled with an air of frustration.

Katy shook her head, her dirt-encrusted hair swaying from side to side. "No, it's not. It's simple. We need to be strong. We need to stand on our own and survive. We don't need the others. We just need to learn how to be stronger than anyone or anything else."

Her brother frowned. "And how do you expect us to do that?"

The small girl shrugged, then stared wide-eyed over Bobby's shoulder. "I don't have an answer to that problem yet. However, what I do know is that, right now, we need to run!"

Bobby turned his head in the same direction and quickly rose to his feet as he saw a pack of hungry-looking dogs stalking their way out of the undergrowth further along the road.

Is this to be my life now? Bobby thought to himself as deceitful bracken lashed him across his protective arm. *Am I just going to spend my time running from one thing after another?* He leapt over a fallen tree and plunged further on into the dense undergrowth.

The dogs were in hard pursuit having emerged up the path between the children and the campsite. The siblings had quickly deduced that to stay out in the open would have been suicide — the lithe dogs would have been upon them by their second or third footfall — so they had plunged into the scrubby woodland by the side of the road, hoping that it would prove more of an obstruction to the hounds than it did to them.

So far they seemed to have been correct.

But, only just.

When the children had been pursued a few days previous by the squad of constructs, they had had speed and agility on their side. The golems may have been relentless, but they had been big, bulky and relatively slow. So it had been possible for the siblings to put space between them and their pursuers, allowing them the opportunity to hide. The dogs, however, were far more fleet of foot and seemingly in desperate need of a quick, nourishing meal. So it was that they barked, yowled and yipped as they plunged through the dense woodland in pursuit of their quarry, seemingly snapping at the children's heels.

Bobby thought there were seven in total. He had managed a cursory headcount as they had set off at a cracking pace, desperate not to end up as a canine snack, but for all he knew there could be more, there could be less.

He prayed for the latter.

His ears were full of just three noises:

the baying of the dogs, the crashing of his feet and the pounding of his heart, as Katy and he emerged into an opening surrounded by a copse of trees.

Completely surrounded by a copse of trees.

The children frantically scanned the densely treacherous plants that seemed to corral them in for their pursuers. There was no way out save the way that they had entered.

And that way was now blocked.

One by one, the dogs slunk in through the same small gap in the trees through which the children had emerged. The wild canines' heads were low; their hackles were raised. An ominous, rumbling growl seemed to echo through the small clearing as the hunters ascertained just how much of a threat their prey would be. Not taking their eyes off the dogs, Bobby and Katy bent down and picked up the only weapons to hand, a pair of stout, arm-long branches. The children hefted them in their hands, testing the weight and simultaneously showing the dogs that they were not going to go down without a fight.

The dogs did not care.

They launched at the children.

Some years ago, his father had been commissioned to turn a particular piece of wood into a vase. One of the villagers of Irlingbury had found the piece of timber whilst out foraging for food in the nearby woods. It had been of quite a size, with a rich grain running through its middle. Rather than doing as many would and simply hacking it to pieces for fuel, they had brought it to Howard and asked him to make a vase in which to hold spring flowers. They had decided that they wanted something of beauty in their life.

Bobby had sat in his father's workshop as his father, in turn, had sat and stared thoughtfully for a long time at the piece of wood, occasionally turning it over in his hands, his eyes tracing the curves of the grain. Then, with a resolute nod, the woodworker had set about carving, shaving and hollowing out the timber until, some hours later, a beautiful vase sat on his workbench. It was a vibrant mix of varying shades of browns, tans and yellows. Swirling patterns spiralled around its body and whorls bloomed from their midst, drawing the on-looker's eye.

To put it simply, it was perfection.

When Bobby asked him how he had known how to produce such a gorgeous piece, his father replied, "Instinct. I studied what was in front of me before committing myself. Then, when I was sure I had all the details in my head, I acted purely on instinct. It is something you should apply to all walks of life. If you correctly link your eyes and your heart, your path will always be true."

These words echoed through his head as the wild dogs loped across the clearing. His eyes quickly scanned the situation in front of him. Four of the dogs were small and wiry. These were the ones who led the charge, their nimble bodies drawing speed quicker than their comrades. They would reach Bobby and Katy first. Behind them were two medium-sized canines. These looked older, more powerful. Their bulky muscles rippled on their shoulders as saliva dripped from their sharp teeth. Then, finally, the largest of the pack ran at the rear, but his size and powerful frame suggested that he would not stay there. As the smaller dogs snapped and harried their prey, he would stride through on his four sure paws before closing his powerful jaws around their future lunch's neck.

In short, Bobby surmised that they would have to fend off the smaller dogs first whilst preventing them from doing any damage before the heavier brutes came in to finish the job.

He had no idea how Katy and he would succeed. The odds were totally overwhelming.

Mind you, they had survived a pitched battle with a battalion of constructs…

Bobby heard himself scream in rage as he swung his improvised weapon at the lead attacker. His stout branch connected with its brown muzzle and the dog yelped in surprise as it swerved off to the left, colliding with its similar-sized counterpart. Bobby continued to thrash and beat at the two smaller dogs, before swinging a roundhouse blow into one of the medium-sized dogs that had approached what it considered to be his unprotected flank. The dog snarled as the blow struck it alongside its tattered ear before lunging forward once more, this time accompanied by the two smaller hounds. Bobby found himself edging backwards to the wall of undergrowth as he swung increasingly more desperate blows at the snapping and snarling teeth that were drawing closer and closer. A quick glance to his right showed him that Katy was in a pretty much similar situation.

His heart finally sank when he felt sharp twigs and dry leaves brush up against his back.

It was then that the largest of the wild dogs launched straight towards him.

At first, Bobby screamed in abject terror at the sight of the deadly teeth plunging through the snarling pack towards his face. He then screamed in utter surprise as the dog flew across the clearing, where it remained pinned against a tree by a thundering horizontal torrent of water.

The other dogs judged quite rightly that their tasty meal was suddenly not worth the effort and, yelping in fright, they scattered as their pack leader squirmed against the forceful tsunami. As the dogs bolted, Bobby's eyes followed the pounding water back to its source and gaped in amazement. A woman with long dark hair was walking confidently into the clearing, her arm outstretched and the water miraculously flowing from her painted fingernails. She was dressed in what could only be described as a stylish manner: red leather trousers that fitted her form perfectly and a long flowing black travelling overcoat. Upon her face was a grin of intense enjoyment as she continued to bombard the helpless dog with her impossible water.

Eventually, the dog went completely limp and the woman ceased her bombardment, allowing it to fall lifelessly to the forest floor. She strode across the clearing, peered down at the deceased canine and poked it with her glossy boot. Seemingly satisfied with her work, she turned toward the two children.

Bobby reached out to Katy with a protective hand but his sister pushed it away, confidently walking over to the stranger, her face radiant with admiration. "Wow!" she breathed. "That was amazing!

"Can you teach *me* how to do it?"

The woman crossed her arms and smiled down at the girl who stood brazenly in front of her. "Well, aren't you the cutest little button?" Her voice was rich and her diction was unlike anything that Bobby had ever heard before. It oozed confidence. She stepped towards Katy and hunkered down. As she did, Bobby noticed that small flames flickered mischievously in her pupils. "Most people would run away from me, but not you." Reaching out one of her finely manicured hands, the woman ran her fingers through Katy's knotted hair. "But look at this," she tutted. "We really ought to do something about it." As she spoke, droplets of water eddied out from her fingers and wove in and out of the child's dirty hair, cleaning and unknotting the locks.

"You know," she seemed to muse to herself as water droplets ran along Katy's hair, washing out the accumulated grime, "I could take you to a grand palace where beautiful servants would pamper you and groom you. They would make you feel like true royalty. How about a bath in nice, hot water? Would you like that? You poor little thing, you look like you haven't had a decent soak in… well, forever."

"We had a bath in a pond the other day," Katy informed the stranger. "After some constructs chased us. We were seriously stinky."

The woman's red lips curled up in a genuine smile as she raised a slim eyebrow. "A quick dip with aquatic wildlife is no substitute for a nice warm soak, trust me."

When she seemed satisfied that Katy's hair was dirt-free, the curious woman snapped her fingers and the water evaporated, leaving Katy's hair the cleanest that it had been in a long time. "Much better," the woman mused. "Far more fitting."

"Fitting for what?" Katy asked.

"Why, fitting for a student of course," the stranger smiled. "You did say that you wanted to *learn*, didn't you?"

Katy's head rapidly bobbed up and down in excitement.

The woman held out her hand. "Well, come on, then. Let's go." She made to walk away and Katy made to follow, before pausing. She turned to Bobby. "Come on," she encouraged. "Let's go."

The boy just stood with his mouth agape. "What? Are you serious?"

Katy nodded. "Absolutely. Don't you see? Imagine what we can learn."

"Katy, we don't know this woman. Just because she rescued us from a pack of wild dogs doesn't mean that we can *trust* her. We don't even know her name."

There was a sense of movement from the edge of the clearing which resolved itself into the form of Claw, the vampire. Scowling out from under his dark hood, he growled, "Bobby's right. You *can't* trust her. And as for her name, it's Asherah. She's one of the Fallen, and she's trouble."

The Fallen peered at the vampire with what appeared to be a vague curiosity. "Have we met?" she asked, tapping a manicured nail against her chin. "Your face is vaguely familiar, but I don't recall all," she waved her hand dismissively at his cloaked attire, "…*this.*"

Claw started to circle slowly towards Bobby, not once taking his eyes off the woman in front of him. The boy started to feel that he regarded her to be far more dangerous than the dogs she had just despatched. "Just the once. In Lancaster. You were leeching off a friend of mine before you tried to destroy his city."

Asherah clicked her fingers in recognition. "Oh yes, I remember now. You were the quiet one. Quite young, from what I recall. And I must say, that's really a harsh accusation you're throwing around there."

"You tried to get the entire city to commit suicide."

"I was in a bad place."

"From what I've heard, that seems to be a permanent state of residence for you."

"You listen to me, *little one*, when you've been around and done as much as I have, life tends to throw you an innumerate amount of curveballs. I can't help it if I'm just in the habit of picking them up and throwing them right back."

"Causing collateral damage in the process," Claw snapped.

"Then people should learn to duck." Asherah let out a deep sigh. "Anyway, enough of this. Come on, Katy," she held out her hand to the small girl, "let's go."

To Bobby's horror, his sister made to head off with Asherah, but before the eight-year-old could place her hand into that of the Fallen, Claw slipped between the two of them. "I can't let you do that," he growled.

The Fallen gave a disgruntled groan. "Oh, for goodness sake, will you just go away."

"I'm not letting you take the girl."

"But she wants to come with me. I can teach her so much."

"Of that, I have no doubt, but that doesn't mean that she should learn it."

Asherah looked around the vampire to Bobby's sister. "You see what he's doing, Katy? He's manipulating you, just like the Children of Cain have always manipulated humanity. They go off on their pointless little quests, dragging people along and eventually getting them killed. I heard what happened to the other two. Do you want to end up like them? Or do you want to be so powerful that no one can push you around anymore?"

"You're twisting things."

"Like hell I am!" Asherah erupted, her cool facade slipping. "I've watched your lot over the years, lurking in the shadows, thinking that you're so superior. Don't forget that while I was in Lancaster, I spent time with Samuel. He told me about how you and yours were constantly jerking his chain, getting him to do what you wanted whilst always keeping him in the dark. You used him like you use everyone else."

"Don't you dare talk about Sam! You betrayed him when you threw your lot in with Kanor."

"Well, it's not like he's going to complain now, is he? Samuel's dead."

Claw shook his head violently. "No. He's out there. I'll find him."

Asherah threw back her head and cruel laughter brayed from her mouth. "And there he is, the fanatical zealot dragging all those around him on a futile quest for his *Man of Virtue*. The prophecy is a lie! There is no Virtuous Man and, if there was, it definitely isn't Samuel. He's dead." She paused and the flames in her pupils flickered slightly as a melancholy filled her voice: "I was with him when he died."

Claw shook his head again. "You're lying. Just like you always do. You'd been sent Beyond before the day he was supposed to have died. It was the day that Lucifer and Abaddon fought at All Saints; the day the devices were detonated in Israel. I'd never forget that day. No one who witnessed it would — the utter devastation."

Asherah's lips curled up just a fraction. "Your little gang never really *got* him, did you? Like I said, jerking his lead this way and that, like a little puppy to play with one minute, then kick the next. Samuel was far more than any of you could ever have envisaged. You never truly saw just how resilient he was. Yes, I was sent Beyond, but who do you think came and saved me? Who do you think kept a promise he had made when he was holding me in his arms when everyone else had rejected me? Samuel kept his promise. He came for me. Then, no sooner had we set foot in this new creation…"

"So how *did* he die?" Claw butted in. "Who killed him?"

"Who do you think? Who wiped out almost everything that was beautiful about this insignificant piece of rock drifting through the blackness of space?"

The vampire stood silently as the enormity of what the Fallen had said sunk in.

Asherah nodded to herself. "So you see, your little quest is in vain. The prophecy was false. There is no Virtuous Man; there is only the Black Dragon. As a result, it's up to each and every one of us to stand on our own two feet and make the best of the cards we've been dealt. And," she smiled, "if that means you have to play with a marked deck to gain the upper hand, so be it." She held out her hand to Katy.

"You still can't take her."

The Fallen took a deep breath and a sly smile formed on her lips. "And you really think you can stop me?" It was then that Bobby heard a tune start to drift across the clearing. It took him a while to realise from where it was coming, but it began to dawn on the teenager that Asherah was humming the lilting melody. It grew in intensity, filling his head and making him feel weak at the knees. He slumped to the forest floor, as did Claw. His heart thumped in his chest and clouds parted as sunlight streamed in on the undeniable fact that the woman standing in front of him was the most wonderful person ever to have walked the face of the planet. How could he have doubted her? Of course she had his best interests at heart.

She shook her head and the song ceased.

Bobby felt empty and discarded.

"Cool," Katy whispered.

"It is rather. Come with me and I can teach you how to do that and so much more. You'll never be a victim again; never be a pawn in someone else's game."

Katy slipped her hand into Asherah's. The Fallen clicked her fingers and, with a loud snap, the two of them vanished.

Chapter Three

For a while, Bobby and Claw walked in silence.

Katy's gone: the teenage boy thought to himself. She wasn't next to him, hitting at plants with a makeshift sword. She wasn't complaining that she was hungry, even though she had just eaten. She wasn't crying out that she wanted to be bigger and stronger, able to take down those that bullied and oppressed her.

Because she was gone.

Ever since his father had placed her gently in his arms, she had always been there. She had been his responsibility. When their father had been taken ill after their mother had died, Bobby had become the one to watch over his younger sibling.

He had been the one to feed her, wash her, look after her.

To keep her safe.

He had failed.

What had happened? Why had she gone with Asherah, a complete stranger? Why had she turned her back on him?

It was because she thought I was weak. She thought that I was going to go running after Claw on his quest for the Virtuous Man. Bobby sighed. Did she really think that he thought more of that so-called quest than he did of her? Did she think that she would get more attention from the female Fallen?

As the two of them walked to where the horses were tied, the boy said, "I want to go after her. I need to rescue Katy."

Claw stood with his back to Bobby. His shoulders rose and fell under the heavy cloak. "Bobby, that's just not possible. You saw how strong Asherah is. That was just a mild taste of her power. I've seen her use it to do much worse."

"But there has to be a way. We can't just abandon my sister."

The vampire ran a gloved hand over his horse, which whinnied softly at his touch. "I'm sorry, Bobby. I need to resume my search for the Virtuous Man. Only when I find him can we end all this once and for all, with the death of Kanor."

Bobby felt his eyes begin to burn with hot tears. "Then she was right. You don't care about anybody else. You and your kind just use us and discard us when we're an inconvenience. You don't mind having us along for the ride, but when things get complicated, you just cut us loose."

"Bobby…" he began.

"No! There's no explanation. You claim to be looking for a Man of Virtue, yet what could be less virtuous than leaving a girl in the hands of a Fallen? Do you think Tigress and Scorpion would leave it like that? What about your friend, Sam? What about him?"

Claw's hood shifted from his horse to the two other riderless mounts then over to Bobby. "Scorp and Tigress would berate me and badger me until we rode off on any excuse to give Asherah a bloody nose. Sam…" He shook his head. "You really remind me of him, you know? A normal person that's been dragged Into a very un-normal world. I hope you meet him someday. I think the two of you would really get on."

"Do you think he's dead?"

The vampire resolutely shook his head. "Not for an instant, and I know one other thing for sure."

"What's that?"

"He'd be telling me that we need to rescue Katy."

They travelled for three solid days. This time, Bobby rode solo and Claw rode with the spare steed tied to his saddle. The first day, for Bobby, was mainly spent overcoming his fear of the beast that carried him through the deserted countryside. As the centres of population became increasingly more sparse, until they were eventually cantering through what could only be described as wilderness, the teenager started to find his rhythm and was able to forget that he was atop an animal that could easily throw him to the ground then trample him under its powerful hooves.

He was helped in overcoming his fear by Claw's methods of distraction. These mainly involved talking. In fact, he talked far more than Bobby had ever considered him capable of. When there had been the three Children of Cain, it had normally been the garrulous Tigress who had filled the silences, with the mute Scorpion not saying a word and Claw seemingly comfortable to let the fiery redhead take centre stage. Now though, he talked almost incessantly, mainly about things which had happened in the dim, distant past. It was as if something inside of him had been uncorked and hundreds of years of memories had been released.

He described the world in which he had grown up as a mortal, the one where he had been reborn as a vampire. He talked about modes of transport that hadn't existed for over a thousand years. He waxed lyrical about famous people known as *celebrities,* of whom the whole world seemed to be in awe. He pooh-poohed politicians and world leaders who failed to stop a crisis in a far-off land that led to a whole country being destroyed by things that he described as *nuclear devices.*

"The Damascus Accord was a front for those in power pretending that they had smoothed things over," he explained. "They realised that their voters wanted the matter resolved so they made it appear that they had done just that. There was this famous shot of the American president standing on the steps of the conference centre waving a sheet of paper in his hand." He snorted in amusement.

"What is it?"

"Funny thing was, they found him dead in bed the morning that the devices went off in Israel. When they performed an autopsy on his body, it appeared that his heart had been burned to a crisp. No one ever claimed responsibility, but I have my suspicions."

He then neatly diverted the topic onto something called the *Infinity Gauntlet* and rambled on unintelligibly for three hours about a guy named *Thanos.*

Bobby glazed over at that bit. He felt a bit guilty at doing so as Claw was *really* enthusiastic about the whole thing, but to the teenager from a world without mass entertainment, it just sounded like words, words, words.

Eventually, when they reached a suitable place to rest the horses, Bobby asked his travelling companion, "So, where are we actually going? Do you know where Asherah has taken Katy?"

Claw heaved the saddles off their steeds and settled the horses as he said, "I have a fair idea where she is. The Fallen has a palace, for want of a better word, over by a place called Sewell. Have you heard of it?" When Bobby shook his head, the vampire continued. "It used to be a small village next to a huge reservoir that was constructed in order to supply water to the local area, Irlingbury included. Asherah set up camp there as water is her elemental power."

"I remember you saying so before the battle at Rishton. She used it to drive off the dogs."

Claw nodded and began to lay a fire. "Remember, Asherah and Asmodeus are fallen angels. This makes them incredibly powerful. Far more so than Kanor's constructs. They used to exist in the Realm known as Heaven. There are two other realms: the Physical realm, which is this one, and Beyond."

"She mentioned that before, didn't she?"

Claw nodded. "It's a hell dimension. A terrible place, by all accounts. Asherah and Asmodeus both wound up there."

"How?"

"They were killed here in the Physical Realm. But I'm digressing somewhat. As I said, Asherah chose Sewell so she could be next to the water there because it's her element."

Bobby pondered this for a moment. "And Asmodeus' element is the lightning that shot from his hands when he attacked you."

Claw struck a flint, causing the tinder to spark into life. He stretched his neck and Bobby could hear the tendons pop. "Correct. And it hurts like a bitch. Each angel has their own ability, their power. What we need is one to use theirs to defeat Asherah."

"And that's where we're going? To find

another angel?"

The fire danced in the vampire's eyes as he sat silent for a moment. "He's someone I first met a long time ago." He pulled a face.

"What is it?"

"We didn't exactly hit it off." Claw poked the fire with a stick and embers rose into the night air. "But he's a good person and incredibly powerful. More so than Asherah, in fact. As long as he agrees to use his powers."

"What's this angel's name?"

"It's Michael. And he's not just *any* angel. He was the Archangel in charge of the army of Heaven."

On the evening of the third day of travel, Bobby found himself standing at the bottom of a craggy hill. Up above, the moon was but a thin sliver of silver, like a bow readying itself to fire an arrow into the dark.

"So, he's up there?"

Claw had removed his cowl and nodded. "As I said, Michael keeps himself to himself. He doesn't like visitors." The vampire paused as if recalling a previous visit. "He *really* doesn't like visitors."

Bobby nodded and, as they began the steep climb up the winding, overgrown path, Claw filled him in somewhat with regard to the former general of Heaven's army. On the day of the Divergence, there had been a huge battle between the angels and the constructs. It had been brutal and had not gone well. When Kanor had risen, Michael had refused to get involved and had walked away from his duties. The rest of the angels had retreated to the Heavenly Realm, leaving him here on Earth, an outcast.

"As you can see," Claw said, pointing out vague movement of large white blobs in the gathering gloom, "he turned his hand to other ventures."

"Are… are they sheep?"

"Immortal beings have to have a hobby," Claw grimaced. "Something to while away the long, tedious years of bitter regret."

As Bobby peered up at the not insignificant flock wandering aimlessly around past an old, gnarled tree, he became aware of a sudden change in the air around him. He shivered as the long grass upon which the sheep were munching began to sway back and forth. "Wind's getting up," he observed. "We'd better get a move on."

There was the smooth sound of Claw drawing his sword. "That's no ordinary wind."

As soon as the vampire had spoken, Bobby felt himself get slapped in the face by an unseen force. He cried out and staggered backwards. It was only the quick reflexes of Claw that prevented him from tumbling back down the hillside. The vampire's arm whipped out and his gloved hand caught the teenage boy by the arm. Bobby forced his head down and tried to resume his footing as an increasingly tempestuous gale circled around them. As the wind blew and howled, it seemed to gather up debris from the ground: sticks, grass, mud, stones. These snapped left and right, pummelling the two intruders, smacking into their shoulders, scratching at their faces. Claw stood firm footed and swiped around with his sword, his preternatural speed managing to bat away the worst of the debris. He began to doggedly advance up the path, pulling Bobby along in his wake, protecting the boy from the worst of the onslaught.

The wind began to shriek and, in its high-pitched wailing, the two of them could make out voices demanding that they leave, that they return to where they came from. Bobby blinked against the elemental force and, as he did so, he witnessed the most incredible of things. The debris that had been snatched up from the hillside was forming into the bodies of beings that stood in the maelstrom to block their way. Claw struck out with his sword at the beings made from leaves, grass, sticks and stones, trying to hack them apart, but every time his sword appeared to strike home, the matter from which the beings were fashioned would simply spread apart, ensuring that the sword just swept through without causing any damage. The matter would then resume its form, creating a hazard through which Bobby and Claw could not pass.

Bobby felt something hard pressed into his hand. It was the vampire's sword. Unable to speak across the howling wind, Claw pressed his hand firmly around Bobby's, the message clear: "Don't drop it." Then, he reached to his belt and unlatched his long whip. Flexing his arm, the weapon cracked out through the storm and lashed itself around a branch of the old tree under which the sheep stood, still quietly grazing as if nothing was happening, just a short distance away. Bobby felt a brief squeeze of warning, then the world was a blur and the two of them were through the maelstrom and standing under the tree, Claw's whip coiled around his wrist. As Bobby bent over to get his breath, he watched the wind finally drop, all the debris it had fashioned into guards falling lifelessly to the ground.

The two companions were about to resume their journey up the hill when there was a clanking of heavy bells as the somewhat ramshackle flock of unkempt sheep wandered purposefully onto the track. Bobby tried to walk around them, but the flock shuffled as one in front of him, blocking his path. He looked over to Claw for help.

The vampire couldn't help but smile as

he waded into the morass of damp-smelling fleece and grabbed one of the animals by its curled horns, intending to heave it out of the way. However, he swore loudly as another member of the ovine group butted him re-soundingly on the rear. "Seriously? Attack sheep?"

The vampire and the boy were now completely surrounded by the flock and were unable to move forward or even retreat back down the hill. They appeared to be drifting helplessly in an ocean of wool and bleating.

"At least," came a deep voice from higher up the track, "they're not fatal. Well, not usually."

Bobby managed to force himself around so that he could see the source of the voice. Up above them stood a tall, broad-shouldered, dark-skinned man. He was dressed in simple homespun clothing and his tightly curled hair was wild and un-kempt. "Not usually?" the boy called.

"Maurice there," the man pointed with a sturdy staff at the largest of the sheep, "does tend to have a foul temper, so you would be best not to provoke him. I'm going to call them off now and you're going to walk back down that hill. Don't come back."

"Michael! Wait!" Claw called out. "We need your help."

"I can't help anyone. You of all people should know that."

"You're our only hope."

Bobby noted that the Archangel raised an eyebrow. "You quoting one of your favourite films at me?"

"It's Asherah," the vampire continued, ignoring the comment. Instead, he gestured around the cohort of sheep to Bobby. "She's got his sister. We can't let her corrupt the girl, can we?"

"I can't help you."

"Please," Bobby called out, "at least let us up. We've travelled so far. We need somewhere to stay for the night."

Michael peered down through the gloom. "How old are you, boy?"

"About fourteen, I think. I'm not sure."

"The last time I helped a young lad, it did not go well."

"We can't live in the past, though."

"But it does have a habit of haunting us."

In his head, Bobby saw Cutter transform into the deadly Shadow Wraith. "That I certainly know, sir. However, we mustn't let those ghosts determine our future, must we?"

The Archangel leaned heavily on his staff. He nodded, opened his mouth and let out a deep braying noise. The sheep dissipated and wandered off, presumably to go back to their grazing. He turned and stalked back up the path.

Bobby and Claw exchanged glances and followed.

Atop the craggy hillside stood a small, precisely fashioned hut constructed from intricately hewn timber. In a little garden by the porch, rows of regimented vegetables stood to attention. "You can take the general out of Heaven…" Claw murmured.

"That life is far behind me now."

"Tell that to your carrots."

"If you're going to criticise my agricultural expertise, you can walk right back down that path."

Bobby stepped forward. "We're sorry, sir," he apologised. "It's just it's been a very long journey and we are somewhat drained. Both physically and emotionally."

The Archangel nodded. "The Lady of the Sea can do that to people. She sweeps in like a tsunami and devastates all around her." He glanced at the vampire, then back to the boy. "I was about to make a meal. Would you care to help?"

"You know I can't cook," Claw protested.

A smile formed on Michael's face. "That's okay then, as I wasn't asking you." He turned back to Bobby. "You know what to do with a carrot?"

"Since I was half my height."

The smile travelled up to the dark-skinned man's eyes and, for just an instant, Bobby was sure that he had seen the twinkling of flames in his black pupils before he motioned for the boy to follow him into the cabin. Inside, a table was already laid out with numerous precisely placed vegetables ready to be peeled, chopped and cooked.

Propped up against a wooden beaker and standing guard over the ingredients was a small, tattered doll that had been fashioned from scraps of material. Bobby was about to ask about this curious anomaly when the Archangel enquired, "So, is Don Quixote still chasing windmills?"

Bobby frowned and picked up a short knife with which he started to prepare a bowl of the orange-coloured vegetables. "I don't…"

The Archangel chuckled warmly and peered out of the window at the vampire sitting resolutely by himself on a stool on the porch. "It's okay. It's an old reference. Is he still on his quest?"

"For the Virtuous Man?" Bobby nodded and thoughtfully sliced up the carrots as Michael shredded some sort of leafy green. "He's looking for a man called Sam Spallucci. Tigress and Scorpion seemed to think he was dead though."

"I'm sure they do." Michael's knife paused mid-stroke. "Although, I believe you just used a past tense there…"

Bobby's head bobbed up and down in

three short jerks. "A few days ago. We were ambushed by a squad of constructs led by Asmodeus. Scorpion was killed in battle and Tigress…" The image of the redheaded vampire's immolation filled Bobby's head. He fought back hot tears.

Michael nodded. "I understand." He slid the chopped leaves into a cooking pot and began to prepare an onion.

"I met Spallucci twice, you know?"

"When?"

"The first time was at his mother's funeral. The second was when he had been called in to investigate something that had happened in my church."

Bobby frowned. "Your church?"

The Archangel's knife hovered over the half-sliced onion. "His job was to work out why unusual things happened. I had been sent to watch over a boy a few years older than you. As a result, I was posing as a curate…" He paused when he spotted Bobby's confusion at the unfamiliar word. "That's an assistant priest at a church." When Bobby nodded at this, he continued. "Well, something *very* unusual happened and the senior priest at the church, the vicar, called Spallucci in." He looked down at the onion as if he could see the scene replaying on the allium's white flesh.

"What happened?"

"I'm not entirely sure. Something far more curious than what he had come to investigate." He finished his dicing of the onion and slid it into the pot. "How are those carrots?"

Bobby showed him the chopped root vegetables.

"Perfect. Let's put them in the pot and see how our friend is doing outside, shall we?" He adjusted the heat in the fireplace and headed out onto the porch, Bobby at his heel.

Claw was still sitting on the small stool, apparently peering out into the dark. "That's quite a drop there," he motioned to the edge of the hill, just past the hut. "You lost any of your sheep over it?"

"They have far more sense than most people do. They intuitively stay away from danger rather than apparently seek it out."

The vampire rose from his seat in one

fluid motion and casually wandered over to the edge of the precipice. He peered over and gave a low whistle. "Yep, quite a drop."

"You want to be careful," Michael warned, his voice somewhat tense. "You don't want to fall over there."

Claw's shoulders gave a quick shrug. "Not too much of a biggie. Vampire, remember?" He gave the sheer drop one last look then asked, "What the hell are you doing here?"

Michael groaned and made to reply, but the vampire cut him short.

"No! Don't! No feeble excuses. You're the general of Heaven's army. You dwelt in the Sanctuary of Yahweh. You looked upon the Presence of God! Why on earth are you sat on the top of a ruddy hillside, tending sheep? Why aren't you leading the world against Kanor?"

The Archangel swallowed. "Because I don't want to see any more pointless deaths. Every time I meddle, people die. *Good* people."

"You could defeat his construct army. You beat them at Megiddo."

"You weren't there." Michael's head bowed as if he were studying the ground in front of him, his voice low, barely audible. "The cost was too high. Gabriel... the thought of where he ended up when he used the Potency. That place is a hell." He drew in a deep breath and straightened himself up. "Besides," he waved a hand around him, at his hut, his garden and his sheep, "this is what I am now. I have no powers. They died many years ago."

Bobby saw one of Claw's eyebrows rise. "Really? And what was that down on the hillside? Just smoke and mirrors?"

The Archangel just shrugged.

"You can't hide up here. The world needs you. *We* need you."

"As I said, I have no powers anymore. Only the occasional parlour trick."

The vampire slowly shook his head, then gave a glance over the edge of the hillside. "I really don't believe that. Not one bit." He turned and his eyes fixed firmly on Bobby. The next thing the boy knew, he was sailing down over the side of the cliff.

Bobby had been told before, when he was small, that when you faced death everything went slow and your whole life flashed in front of you. One day, a farmer had come to his father to trade for a new ladder. His old one had broken whilst he had been trying to repair the thatch above his front door. One minute, the farmer had said, he had been at the top of the ladder, reaching out to wedge some new straw into the gap in the roof, the next, he was standing on nothing and he was aware that he was falling, the top rung of the ladder clutched in his hand. "It was the most bizarre experience. As I fell backwards, down to the porch below, all that I had done passed in front of my eyes: every birth of my five children; the day of my marriage; the time I got caught snatching fish from old man Harper's backyard; the time I pissed my pants when my mother took me out into the roughs to collect berries. All those and many more casually wandered past my eyes and waved hello at me. It must have taken as much time as it would walking to Orchester, yet in reality, I crashed to the floor in the blink of an eye."

He shook his head and rubbed his dirty hand against his stubbled chin. "Everything moved so slow. So slow indeed."

Bobby, as he felt the wind scream past him whilst the ground below opened its deadly arms to catch his falling body, saw none of this. There were no reassuring images from his past to comfort a possible entrance through the doors to the afterlife. There were no feelings of regret for mistakes or mishaps from his previous years.

There was just terror. Complete, absolute, terror.

He was initially aware of just two things: the rushing air buffeting up past his flailing arms; his mouth open in a piercing scream.

And then there was a white blur shooting down towards him and he was snatched away from becoming a messy tangle of squished body parts on the valley floor below. His mouth gaped and flapped as he turned to see what held him, but no words came at the sight of the white-garbed, winged being with radiant skin and fiery eyes that held him tightly in its arms.

They rose up the face of the cliff and the being alighted gently on the grassy top of the hillside. It carefully lowered Bobby to the floor before bending down and asking in a familiar voice, "Are you okay?"

"Michael?" Bobby reached out with a shaking hand to touch the Archangel's transformed attire, but his fingers paused just before they met the fabric.

"Go on. It's okay."

The vestment felt unlike any sort of clothing he had ever touched. There was no trace of a weave or a stitch. The silken material slipped between his fingertips. He gazed up into his saviour's face. "Your eyes…" he breathed. "They're on fire."

Michael nodded. "This is my true form. Well, my true anthropomorphic form." He smiled as Bobby frowned. "A form that looks *human*. Technically, angels are beings of energy, which is why we can change appearance should we so desire. This is how I normally look when I interact with others."

"Like Asmodeus and Asherah do?"

Michael nodded again. "When they were in Heaven, they looked like me. But without this." He tapped at a burnished gold plate of armour that hung moulded to his chest.

"Because you're a soldier."

"*Was* a soldier."

Bobby ran a finger over the breast-plate. It felt unusually warm to the touch, a slight vibration running through the metal. "Please. We could really use your help. You're the only person I've met who could be a match for Asherah. If Tigress and Scorpion were still alive, we may have stood a chance. But now…"

The Archangel sighed and looked from the boy to the silent vampire, to his crude cottage.

"Okay. But first, we eat and, as we eat, we talk tactics."

Chapter Four

It was decided that Bobby, Claw and Michael would set off for Sewell early the next morning. It had been mutually agreed that, although the Archangel and the vampire could have travelled through the night, Bobby was in desperate need of a good night's sleep. Michael had made up his simple bed, bade Bobby a good night and retreated out of the small bedroom.

The exhausted teenager threw himself onto the bed and didn't even make it under the covers before sleep consumed him.

Not that it was very restful.

As he fell into a deep sleep, there was at first a peaceful dream waiting for him. Bobby found himself walking through a wide meadow. Small, red flowers that he did not recognise bloomed through the stems of wild grass. In front of him, skipping in the bright sunlight was Katy. She was singing to herself and, every now and then, she would stop and pick some of the flowers, bunching them together into a small posy. Bobby smiled to himself as he followed her through the lush grass.

"Who are they for?" he called out to his kid sister.

Katy bent to add more flowers to the growing bunch. "For Mother, of course, You know how she loves them."

Bobby nodded. Their mother was indeed fond of flowers. "She'll definitely love them," he agreed. "She'll put them in that vase father made for her."

Katy stopped and frowned. "Why would she do that?"

"What else would she do with them?"

The small girl looked down at the flowers. Their scarlet colour was running from the petals, pooling in a viscous puddle at her feet. "These flowers are not for the living," she whispered. "They are for the dead." When she looked back up at Bobby, the boy took a startled step backwards. She was no longer a small, eight-year-old girl, but a young woman. Her long brown hair cascaded down over her cloaked shoulders, framing her pale skin. "I killed her!" this older version of Katy cried as the bone-white moon rose over her shoulder. Then forming her mouth into a hard smile that revealed a pair of sharp fangs, she declared, "She was just the first!"

The vampire Katy leapt forward at Bobby. He turned and fled through the long grass that was stained crimson from the blood of the flowers. The horizon was empty except for one detail toward which he found himself being inexplicably drawn — a familiar, large oak tree. As he approached it, he saw the three females from his previous dream: the child, the woman and the old crone. They nodded as one as he pulled to a halt before them, then seemed to merge into one body before they said, "We are waiting."

Bobby snapped awake, gasping for breath and his limbs tangled in bedclothes.

The bedroom door flew open and Claw was by his side. "Are you okay? We heard shouting."

Bobby's eyes snapped to the open door and saw Michael standing there, concern in his fiery eyes. "It was just a bad dream. Nothing more." He felt the reassuring grip of Claw's cold hand on his shoulder, but the Archangel's eyes were far more cautious. "Is it time to go?"

Claw nodded. "The horses are ready."

Bobby swung his legs over the edge of the bed, then asked, "Why are we riding there? Isn't Michael able to…" He clicked his fingers.

"I'm afraid, that I am somewhat out of practice," the Archangel explained as they walked through the house and out to the waiting horses. "It would be best that I conserve my energy for our encounter with Asherah. Whereas she and Asmodeus have had continual usage of their angelic powers, I…" He held his hand out to his sheep.

Bobby frowned. "But you'll be able to beat Asherah?"

Michael climbed up onto his horse, his

eyes dark. "Let's go and find out, shall we?"

The journey to Sewell took the best part of two days. There was a road that led straight there, but Michael and Claw both agreed that taking the direct route into the heartland of an area dominated by the female Fallen would have been exceedingly hazardous and foolhardy. As a result, they travelled cross-country, picking their way across bleak, abandoned fields, constantly watching the horizon for movement.

The Archangel's dark eyes were fixed firmly ahead as they travelled, his mind clearly elsewhere.

Bobby pulled up even with him as they passed a ruin of red bricks that had once been someone's home. "What was it like?"

Michael turned to face him and raised an eyebrow in question.

"Here," Bobby explained. "Before the Divergence."

The angel nodded and Bobby could see him forming an acceptable answer. "Different," he finally said. "Very different." He shifted in his saddle and the reins tapped against the side of his horse. "By the time of the Divergence, humans had spread all over the planet and had even started to go out into space. They achieved incredible things, bringing the planet back from the brink of ecological disaster; eliminating poverty and hunger. They had entered a golden era.

"At least for a while.

"Some said that it was due to the battle in Wellington between Abaddon and Lucifer, the revelation that they were not alone in the universe. Some said that it was the horror of the obliteration of Israel after the arrogance of the Damascus Accord imploded. Perhaps it was just a natural progression of events. I don't know. Perhaps it was a combination of all of these factors. But, when Kanor rose and the constructs activated, humanity never saw it coming. Half the population of the world was gone overnight, either turned into what they really were or slaughtered by their loved ones. The shockwave of the catastrophe left the rest paralysed in fear, making them easy pickings for the unstoppable army of constructs as they steadily worked their way through the population, carefully culling the herd, thinning them down to a manageable level for their master."

"Why didn't he wipe everyone out completely?"

"I don't know. Perhaps he needed a workforce? Perhaps he just wanted to watch them suffer? Who knows what that dark mind thinks?" The Archangel appeared to shudder and gave a deep sigh.

"Do you think it's possible to defeat Kanor?"

Michael was silent for a short while. "Our friend there," he inclined his head to the cloaked vampire behind them, "seems to think that a mere mortal, this *Man of Virtue*, is the one to overthrow the Black Dragon. Trust me, that's just a pipe-dream. No living being could beat Kanor. He is the most powerful creature who ever walked this planet."

Bobby frowned as he considered the Archangel's words. "You're talking as if you know who he is."

Michael's eyes held Bobby's and the fires burned fiercely in his pupils. "I have my suspicions. Something happened at the battle at Megiddo; after we beat back the constructs. To this day I'm not sure what it was or how it happened. One minute someone I knew was one person, then next he was someone else, someone I had watched him become before."

Bobby frowned. "You're not making any sense."

"You have to remember this, Bobby, before the Divergence hit, Time took a different path. Heaven and the Physical Realm combined to make an eternal paradise. Angels, being creatures of energy, can still recall that. We have two sets of memories that stand side by side. I remember my friend walking up to God Himself and being given his reward for saving us. He was given the highest rank of angels. The rank of Seraph.

"But, I also experienced a reality where that never happened. *This* reality. In *this* timeline, Heaven and the Physical Realm never converged and when I joined my friend at the end of the battle of Megiddo, he became the very entity that he had just slain and, in his hand, that being held the thing that he had used to escape Beyond."

Bobby was about to ask who Michael's friend was when the Archangel's head snapped up and he peered at the far horizon. "Company," he murmured.

Claw's horse drew up next to them. "It's a small squad," he said, motioning to the line of figures in the distance. "Not surprising as we're only a mile or so away now. You think they've seen us?"

The Archangel shook his head. "They're heading away from us. If we keep moving, we'll be there for nightfall. We'll just have to keep our eyes open and," he glared at Bobby, "keep idle chatter to a minimum." Twitching his reins, he cantered his horse off in front of the other two.

"Don't mind him," Claw reassured the boy. "He's just been through a hell of a lot."

"So I noticed," Bobby replied.

Sewell was not what Bobby had expected. Not at all.

At Michael's suggestion, they had left the horses tethered in a small barn on what appeared to be a deserted farm a few minutes' walk outside of the settlement. "We will be more mobile in the town if we enter on foot," he explained. "Should we happen to get split up, we can rendezvous back here."

As they approached the large body of water, signs of civilisation started to become apparent. Cultivated fields filled the land with humans hunched over, hard at work. Not once did anyone stand up to watch the strangers passing by. The three companions rejoined the main road and proceeded with care through an increasingly urban settlement. Bobby gaped at the housing. It was palatial by the standards that he was used to. Along clean, polished streets, freshly painted wooden houses marshalled their approach to the palace that stood before the vast lake.

Bobby sniffed and his forehead wrinkled. "What's that smell?"

A brief smile crossed Michael's face. "Something you're not used to. Cleanliness. The Lady of the Sea is not a fan of filth and squalor. All these people may be her slaves, but she'll want them to… *look their best* in their servitude." He shook his head and let out an exasperated sigh.

At the intersection of every street stood a giant carved pole that was entwined with black and red ribbons. At the base of each were plates of food, tools and carved wooden figures.

"You can take the goddess out of Canaan…" Michael muttered to himself. "Kanor may rule the land," he said to the others, "but have no doubt that this is very much Asherah's own little kingdom. She's still living the glory days of old." He nodded to himself as half a dozen constructs rounded the corner and blocked their way, a Shadow Wraith at their head. "We can use this. Just follow my lead when the time comes."

"You will come with us," declared the Shadow Wraith as it flicked its arm out to one side, forming a cruel-looking curved blade.

"Now, why would we do that?" Michael asked, standing nonchalantly in the middle of the cobbled street as if he were out for a casual stroll. "It's a glorious day. The sun is shining and the air is clear. My fellow travellers and I are just out enjoying the sights."

"Because the Lady of the Sea demands it."

The Archangel smiled and nodded knowingly. "Your mistress has demanded many things over the millennia. She's not always got what she wanted."

"Trust me," the Wraith threatened, "this time she will." He motioned with his blade and the constructs began to march toward the three companions.

Michael stood impassively, his arms by his side.

Bobby looked nervously from the angel to the vampire.

Claw had unclipped his whip.

A slight breeze began to tickle the hairs on the back of Bobby's neck.

When the cohort of golems was about fifty paces away, Michael thrust his hands out in front of him and a sudden blast of air rocketed down the street. Bobby braced himself in order to stand firm as the elemental force sent the constructs tumbling head-over-toe like wooden pins that had been knocked over by a small child. The pinwheeling golems reached out with their arms. Their elastic limbs stretched out to grab the nearest buildings to prevent themselves from being driven all the way down the street.

The Archangel kept up his unrelenting attack and, as he did so, began to walk steadily forwards. Bobby and Claw followed behind. As they did, Bobby became aware of a familiar sensation. A pounding one-two beat of feet was rising up from the ground through his feet and then his legs. He glanced over his shoulder and blanched as he saw a second cohort of constructs approaching behind them.

"We've got a problem!" he managed to yell over the roaring winds just as a clay arm wrapped itself around his middle and yanked him backwards. The road was hard and unforgiving as he collided with the ground. He cried out and tried to pull the smooth, clasping arm away from him, but it continued to coil up his body, wrapping itself around his arms, quickly immobilising him. Bobby tried to struggle as he felt himself being dragged along the floor, but it was no use. Instead, he looked on aghast as both Michael and Claw succumbed to the same sort of attack.

In a few moments, all three of them were coiled in the unforgiving embraces of constructs.

The Shadow Wraith stalked over to them, dusting itself down and stretching itself out. Bobby watched as tears in the fabric of its simulacra of clothing miraculously knitted themselves back together. "As I was saying," it glowered, "you will come with us."

Having no current apparent means of escape, boy, vampire and angel did as they were told.

If it hadn't been for the mortal dread of impending death, Bobby would have considered himself incredibly lucky to have entered Asherah's palace. As the three of them were frogmarched up the hill from the settlement and in through the wide wooden gates of the large stone building, his breath was taken away, and not just by the constricting coils around his chest.

The immediate inside of the building was a large courtyard that would have been open to the sky had the space above not been covered with brightly coloured fabrics that fluttered gently in a soft breeze, creating a kaleidoscope of hues as the sun above shone through the textile ceiling. More of the tall wooden poles stood sentinel around the courtyard, again entwined with black and red ribbons. The whole area smelt of something incredibly sweet and not unpleasant. Around the edge of the area, draped over piles of cushions or lying on long, plush ornate seats were numerous men and women. Bobby noted that they all had two things in common: they were all incredibly attractive and none of them was wearing much in the way of clothing. They all seemed to have a listlessness to their demeanour and a faraway look in their eyes.

There was movement at the opposite end of the courtyard and a set of rich, blue curtains swept apart at the touch of an unseen hand. Asherah slid into the room. She wore her long dark hair curled up atop her head, exposing her graceful neck. She was adorned in a sleeveless dress of flowing, pearlescent fabric that seemed to glitter in the colours from the awnings above. Her bare arms were stretched out to her sides and water was spiralling around her perfect skin. She smiled warmly as she reached out and let tendrils of water stroke and caress her lounging devotees who murmured contentedly at her touch. As the droplets of water passed from one to the other, each acolyte tried unsuccessfully to reach out and keep in contact with the flowing liquid.

Finally, the Fallen stood in the middle of the room and commanded the constructs, "Release them and leave us."

The Shadow Wraith did not hesitate to bow in submission and walked out of the courtyard, accompanied by his troops.

"Well, well, well," Asherah murmured in her rich voice as she sidled over to Michael. "This truly is a surprise. "I thought you had taken up a life of *shepherding.*" The word was brimming over with distaste.

"It passes the long, fruitless years," the Archangel shrugged. "At the end of the day, they're so much easier to control than people."

"But they're so much harder to bathe." The Fallen stood directly behind him, the fabric of her dress touching his clothes. "You know that I like to keep things fresh and fragrant."

"You seem to be doing a very good job of that. I must say that I'm very impressed at what you've carved out for yourself here."

Asherah placed her chin on Michael's shoulder and leaned the side of her head against his stubbled cheek. "Are you now?" she mused, fire twinkling in her dark eyes. Her manicured hand slid up his arm. "Is that why you so brazenly walked into Sewell? To admire my handiwork?"

"That," he replied, "and to bring the Lady of the Sea a gift." He looked at Bobby and Claw, his eyes pure flame. "Two, in fact."

Bobby felt as if the earth below him had vanished and he was falling without control. When he had been small, he had gone with his mother to play on the riverbank. She had told him not to go far, but he had been insistent that he wanted to watch the water flowing over the pebbles. She had agreed, but had told him to take care as the side of the river was slippy and treacherous. At first, he had stood back from the edge, peering into the rippling water, laughing as it tinkled over the small rocks. But the excitement and the beauty had lured him closer and it wasn't long before he was standing on a muddy outcrop overhanging the babbling brook. Something silver darted underneath him and he was just about to call to his mother that he had seen a fish, when the world around him disappeared and the outcrop gave way, causing him to plummet down into the cold water below. He scrabbled and screamed until he felt the hand of his mother on his arm, pulling him up to safety. For that brief instant, it had felt as if he was going to fall through to the other side of the planet.

His mother, however, was not with him when Michael betrayed him to Asherah.

Bobby felt his stomach lurch as he suddenly found himself trapped and powerless in the lair of one of the most powerful creatures on the planet. He stole a glance at

Claw. The vampire was just standing impassive, motionless.

"And, pray tell," the soft voice of the Fallen purred into the ear of the Archangel as she wrapped a hand around his chest, "why would I want these two… filthy vagrants?"

"Claw is the last of his kind," Michael stated matter-of-factly, his eyes staring straight ahead, "and I believe that the boy could be special."

The manicured hand ceased in its caressing of the Archangel's chest, the Fallen's curiosity obviously piqued. "Special? How?"

"I believe you took his sister?"

Asherah walked around in front of Michael, her eyes studying the teenage boy. Bobby felt like a mouse being sized up by an adder. "She intrigued me. I saw potential in her."

"Well, he is from the same stock. Imagine if you had two of them. Your *own* powerful pair of children. Imagine how useful that could be…"

Bobby frowned as the treacherous angel let the implication hang. He felt like he was missing something here.

The Fallen crossed her slender arms and tapped her red lips with a coloured nail. "Bring the girl!" she snapped, and the devotee closest to the curtained doorway slipped out of the room. He returned shortly with a certain eight-year-old.

"Katy!" Bobby cried out. "Are you okay?"

His sister frowned at him and joined Asherah in the middle of the room. "Why are they here?"

"Apparently, they are a gift. Do you think I should accept them?"

"What if it's a trap?"

"Shall we find out?"

Katy nodded enthusiastically.

The Fallen affectionately ruffled the girl's hair and opened her mouth. At once, the room was filled with a harmonious song that caused the lounging acolytes to commence a deep groaning of longing and desire. Bobby felt his knees weaken and he was about to sink to the floor when another, louder noise cut across the song.

Michael had his right hand raised in the air and, above him, the coloured awnings of the ceiling were in the process of being torn to shreds as a swirling column of air descended from the sky. The air roared through the room, the tempest obliterating any other noise, including the song of the Fallen. Asherah screamed mutely in frustration and opened her mouth wider in an attempt to increase the volume of her song. At the same time, she raised her hands, balls of water forming at her fingertips.

Michael nodded to Claw and, in the blink of an eye, both the vampire and Katy were gone.

Michael sprung to Bobby's side and, as Asherah's elemental power surged across the room, he grabbed the teenager's arm with one hand and clicked the fingers on the other.

Chapter Five

The first thing that Bobby was aware of when they arrived at the rendezvous point was the sound of Katy screaming blue murder. The second was that he was going to be sick. Turning away from the sight of an irate eight-year-old beating seven bells out of a bemused vampire, Bobby leaned against a rough lattice wall of the barn and emptied the contents of his stomach.

"I'm sorry," came the concerned voice of Michael, as he placed a reassuring hand on the boy's back. "The first time is always the worst for humans. Your physical makeup is not exactly designed for teleportation."

Bobby tried to nod but just ended up dry-heaving into the soiled straw. He braced his palms against the wall and forced himself to stand up, taking in long, slow breaths. As his stomach settled, he turned his attention to the commotion on the other side of the barn.

"How dare you kidnap me! Take me back! Right now!"

The teenage boy sighed. "Katy," he said. "Please, calm down. We came to rescue you."

The small girl diverted her anger away from the vampire and towards her older brother. "Rescue me?" she snapped, her hands on her hips. "Why would you think I need *rescuing*? Am I a rabbit in a snare? A fish on a hook? I was exactly where I wanted to be! Did you not see that place? It was a palace, Bobby! A huge palace. I was clean. I was safe. I was respected. I wasn't being dragged off on some fool's errand by," she shot an evil glare at Claw, "people we hardly know."

Bobby tried to rationalise with his furious sister. "But Asherah is one of the Fallen. She is a servant of Kanor. She can't be trusted."

Katy shook her head. "You've got it wrong. All of it."

"How so?"

"She hates Kanor as much as we do. He did something unforgivable and she wants revenge on him. She only pretends to serve him. She says that one day she will turn on him and make him suffer for what he did."

Michael approached the girl. "What did he do?"

"He killed the only man who was ever kind to her, someone who she cared about greatly."

The Archangel shook his head. "Child, she's lied to you. I've known Asherah for an incredibly long time. The only person she's ever cared about in her long, power-hungry existence has been herself."

"No!" All three males in the barn took an involuntary step backwards as the small girl stamped her foot. "You don't know her like I do. She's kind, caring and genuinely interested in me." Her voice dropped to a near whisper and Bobby shuddered as she murmured, "I can be myself around her."

She looked up, tears in her eyes. "Please… Please take me back.

"You'll regret it if you don't."

The Archangel and vampire looked to the teenage boy for a lead.

Bobby frowned. This was not exactly going to plan. Had the Fallen brainwashed his sister? Had she sung her intoxicating song and made the girl believe that the beautiful woman had her best interest at heart?

Or was it something far more sinister?

Back in Orchester, Katy had killed Teller in cold blood, pushing him off a bridge. There had been no hesitation; she had acted on pure instinct. She constantly complained that she wanted to be stronger, more powerful. She was hungering to fight back against those who hurt them. Had she found someone that she believed could teach her the skills that she needed to stand on her own two feet?

Bobby looked at the vampire and the angel. The apprehension on their faces was clearly visible. There was no doubting that they saw the Fallen as trouble, just another soldier of Kanor.

But Katy wasn't them, was she? *Foulness!* Bobby thought to himself, *She's certainly not me, either.* What if she truly had found a path that was right for her?

Who was he to stand in her way?

How *could* he stand in her way?

He looked down into her dark brown eyes, saw a soul that was far stronger than his own and he nodded. Tears welling up in his eyes, he took his sister in his arms and hugged her tight.

"You're suffocating me," she protested.

"I know," he agreed. "And that's why I have to let you go."

Claw and Michael had protested. Lots.

They had claimed that a small girl could not possibly know her own mind, that she was being manipulated by Asherah and that, to take her back to Sewell, was signing her death warrant. However, Bobby had ignored all their words and simply climbed up onto his horse, pulling his sister up behind him.

"We all have to find our own paths," he

said as he guided the black steed out of the barn. "Ours are no longer with you."

The two supernatural beings had stood in silence as the two children had ridden back towards the palace of the fallen angel.

As their horse cantered down the street lined with the poles decorated with ribbons and they approached the grand palace, Bobby didn't feel nervous. Instead, a curious calm came over him. Even when Asherah herself came out to greet them, residents of Sewell lowering themselves completely so that their faces touched the ground, the boy felt neither fear nor anxiety. Instead, he simply helped Katy to dismount and watched as the small girl ran into the arms of the awaiting woman who closed her eyes and held her tight.

After their reunion, Asherah stood and said, "Thank you, Bobby. That can't have been easy for you. I'm sure other influences advised you against such an act."

"Katy needs to make her own decisions." He looked lovingly down at his sister. "She is quite unique."

The Fallen tousled the girl's hair with

finely manicured fingers. "That she is," she mused. "That she is." Then, turning back to Bobby, "But so are you."

The boy on the horse smiled wryly. "No. I'm just… *normal*. There's nothing special about me whatsoever."

Asherah shook her head. "No, far from it. Someone I once knew thought like that. He was wrong, too. Trust me on this, even if you can't on anything else; you are incredibly special.

"And that is why Kanor is obsessed with you."

Bobby frowned and clenched his reins tight, causing the horse below him to stamp its feet in irritation. "What do you mean?"

"He knows you exist, Bobby. He talks about you constantly. I'm not sure why."

The teenager just nodded. What else could he say after discovering that the person who devastated humanity had now set their sights on him?

"Where will you go?" Katy called up from her place at Asherah's side.

Bobby turned the horse around and began his lonely journey. "I'm not sure, he called over his shoulder. But I'll know when I get there."

It was about five days later when he finally crested a hill and saw the lonely silhouette on the horizon. A few hours later and he found himself dismounting in front of the old oak tree from his dream.

Underneath its wide canopy stood the most curious person he had ever lain eyes upon. She was female but seemed to constantly shift form from that of a small girl, to that of a middle-aged woman, to that of a crone so old and haggard, that Bobby was amazed she had the strength to stand.

After settling his horse, Bobby slowly approached the shape-shifting woman. "I'm here," he said. "Now what?"

"We need your services," said the girl.

"We have an important task for you," said the woman.

"We need you to save the one known as Sam Spallucci," said the crone.

Bobby will return in
Bobby Normal and the Black Dragon

A.S.Chambers

Author's Notes

Thank you for buying this, the penultimate story for Bobby in this five-book series. I hope you enjoyed it and were left somewhat hungry for the final outing, *Bobby Normal and the Black Dragon*, which should be out in 2024, shortly before the penultimate Sam Spallucci book, *Sam Spallucci: To Dare The Dragon*.

I wrote this particular novella whilst I was working on *Sam Spallucci: Fury of the Fallen* and, in fact, both Asherah and Claw refer to events in that book when Asherah and Asmodeus descend upon Lancaster. To a certain extent, this was a bit of a happy accident. From *Bobby Normal and the Virtuous Man,* I had started to want to draw the two series together and, when I found myself working on two books which contained the same antagonist, this was a creative dream come true. I could easily lay a few literary easter eggs along the way for the sharp-eyed readers to gobble up and begin to digest as they started to work out how the two evolving plotlines would start to crossover.

As well as Asherah referring to her time with Sam and his promise to save her from Beyond plus Claw's description of the climax of *Fury*, there is also the mention of the Damascus Accord. This is an event that has been gradually percolating away in the background of the Sam Spallucci books like a very bitter pot of coffee. Every now and then Sam will see a news report or a newspaper article about the troubles in the Middle East. If you go back over the first six books and look carefully, you should find at least one in each book. Then in *Fury,* we have Sam and Asherah watching the news as all the politicians meet to sign the Damascus Accord, ending with a politician doing a Neville Chamberlain and waving a piece of paper for "peace in our time". Well, we all know how that turned out, don't we... In *Bobby Normal and The Fallen,* we discover that the politician was, in fact, the American President and that he suffers a gruesome fate as the Accord goes up in smoke with the obliteration of Israel by nuclear devices. Which brings us neatly to *Fallen Angel...*

As I've mentioned numerous times before in varying Author's Notes, *Fallen Angel* is a novel that I have sat waiting to be published. It's a good old magnum opus that will tie all my Spallucciverse works together, culminating in the Divergence. There have been a lot of references to characters and events in the book throughout the Sam Spallucci books and standalone shorts, but the story you've just read probably stands, at the time of writing, as the piece of work from which you can practically touch this sleeping dragon. By the time *Fury* takes place, the events of *Fallen Angel* are well and truly underway with Asherah and Asmodeus actually referring to something they have done which sets the whole ball rolling, so to speak. Then, in *Sam Spallucci: Lux Æterna,* there will be a direct crossover, which Michael refers to as being the second time that he met Sam (have the sharp-eyed readers out there worked out who he was at the funeral of sam's mother?). But this is not the only reference. The Archangel Michael, himself is a central character and we can tell from his current state here that things did not go well for him. Who was the teenage boy that he was supposed to help? What happened there? Then he refers to the battle between the angels and the con-structs and the fate of Archangel Gabriel. Plus, we cannot ignore that he thinks he knows who Kanor actually is, referring to him as someone who fought at the Battle of Megiddo and is the most powerful person on the planet. Any ideas? I'd love to hear them.

Then there is the matter of Sam.

It goes without saying that Sam Spallucci is the lynchpin of my literary universe, so it makes perfect sense that his actions from over one thousand years previous would impact those who live in the Divergent Lands. There is so much that I could say here, including what plans I have in store for Sam and Bobby, but that way many, many spoilers lie. So, I will just leave you with two questions.

Is Sam, as Claw fervently believes, the Man of Virtue?

Is Sam dead?

Again, I'd love to hear your views.

Until next time, take care and keep looking for what lurks in the shadows.

ASC.

About The Author

A.S.Chambers resides in Lancaster, England. He lives a fairly simple life of walking in the countryside, gazing at mountains and rescuing his cat from the net curtains.

He is quite happy for, and in fact would encourage, you to follow him on Facebook, Instagram, TikTok, YouTube, Threads and Twitter.

There is also a nice, shiny website:
www.aschambers.co.uk